HIS LOVE

FIONA DAVENPORT

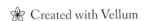

HIS LOVE

Billionaire Justice Kendall thought he was content with his life. Right up until the day he noticed that his neighbor's daughter had become the beautiful woman who was meant to be his. Since then, he waited not-so patiently for her to turn eighteen.

He bided his time by watching over her. When he realized that all she wanted was a baby of her own, he was ready to give her more than just his love.

He'd give her everything.

CHAPTER 1

JUSTICE

"Blair." I nodded to the young girl shuffling up to the elevator in her school uniform. Her long blonde hair was pulled away from her face in a high ponytail, giving her no way to hide the pink blush that bloomed on the apples of her cheeks. She glanced up shyly with her big, blue eyes and bit her plump bottom lip.

Fuck. I had to clench my hand into a fist so that I didn't tug her lip from between her teeth and bite it myself. Her sweet looks always tested my control around her. It didn't help that she was practically the poster girl for a naughty school-girl costume. Her shyness only added to the innocent picture and completed the vision of every man's wet dream.

Despite being only seventeen, Blair Gleason had

the body of a woman. I'd barely noticed my neighbor's daughter over the years until one day when she was sixteen, we'd bumped into each other at the elevator, just like today—just like we do every day now. I'd greeted her without giving her much attention, but then she'd dropped her backpack and everything had spilled out around her feet. She'd spun around and bent over, giving me a perfect view of her lush, round ass in plain, white cotton panties.

I was instantly hard as a fucking rock and couldn't keep my eyes from drifting down her shapely legs. Even with all her curves, she was still a tiny thing. She was at least a foot shorter than my six-foot-five height, which meant I towered over her. With my muscular frame, I practically dwarfed her, but I immediately knew we would fit together perfectly. Blinking rapidly and taking a few deep breaths, I scolded myself for lusting after a child. I was only a few years shy of being twenty fucking years older than her. The silver streaks at my temples and peppered throughout my goatee were a reminder of that whenever I looked in the mirror. I held in a frustrated groan and hurried to help her pick up her things. But when she straightened and slung her bag over her shoulder again, it thrust out her chest and made it impossible not to notice her big tits and how they bounced when she shifted from foot to foot.

My eyes swept over her from head to toe, taking in the sight of the woman she'd turned into all of a sudden. She'd lost the softness of her baby face, but her lips were still bee-stung and puffy. Lips that New York high society women spent thousands of dollars trying to achieve with collagen. Lips that would make a porn star jealous because they would look so fucking perfect wrapped around a cock. Her neck and shoulders were slender, her waist small, but the swell of her hips made it clear that she was made for breeding.

To my complete shock, my cock had started leaking come at the thought of being the one to fill her belly. It was the first day of my living hell. I hadn't realized it at the time, but the next two years were going to be my purgatory. It was no less than I deserved for thinking about sinking into her teenage pussy and filling her ripe womb with my seed.

"Hello, Mr. Kendall," she whispered in a return greeting, drawing me out of my reverie. Whenever she blushed and peeked at me through her lashes like that, she made me think of a cute little bunny.

I smiled gently and gave in to the urge to brush my finger lightly over her jaw. "Justice," I scolded her teasingly. "How many times do I have to tell you to call me Justice?" It was just another form of torture. Hearing my name fall from her lips in her musical voice only made me that much more desperate to hear her screaming it while I was eleven inches deep.

"Sorry," she blushed even deeper and smiled sweetly at me, her hands clutching the strap of her bag tightly. "Good morning, Justice."

"How is school?"

Blair shrugged. "I'm glad I'll be graduating this year."

The elevator dinged, and the door slid open. We stepped into the car, and I pressed the button for the lobby before responding. "And what are your plans after graduation?" I infused my tone with curiosity, hiding the fact that I didn't care what she had planned. I already knew what she'd be doing when she graduated, and she'd know soon enough too.

"I don't know." She shrugged and looked up at me through her long, pale lashes. "Daddy wants me to go to one of the Ivy League schools I've been accepted into."

I raised a brow and shoved my hands in my pockets to keep from touching her. "And that's not what you want?" I had to keep the bite out of my voice at the thought of her going away to college.

Blair shook her head. "I've never really wanted to go to college, but I want to work with kids, so I'll probably focus on getting my degree in early childhood development. I've already got a jump start on it since I'm in a program that substitutes some of my high-school classes for college courses"—she ducked her head and shrugged—"My dad won't be happy about it, but I think I'll keep attending Hunter College."

I almost showed my relief by expelling a deep breath. It was good to know I didn't have a fight on my hands about that. If Blair wanted to finish her degree, I would support her completely. But she'd be doing it locally, at a school in New York City, while I kept her busy having my babies. I'd be happy to quiz her on her homework while she bounced on my dick.

Son of a bitch. I shook away the images before I came in my pants like a horny teenager and scared the fuck out of my girl. I mentally shook my head at myself. It was a year later, and I still had no control over my thoughts around her.

Only one more year. Only one more year. I chanted to myself. It wasn't even a full year. Just until the end of May, right before graduation. I could be patient.

"I'm excited about an internship I have for the

school year, though!" I refocused on Blair, hoping to be distracted from my depraved thoughts. Her tone had become animated, and her beautiful face lit up like the Fourth of July. "I guess they had a spot open up in the in-house daycare at K-Corp. Someone reached out to one of my professors, and she recommended me! They are even allowing me to use it as a practicum for one of my classes. I just hope I don't disappoint them."

I already knew about her internship. I'd been the one to facilitate it. Ever since I started paying attention to her, I noticed and heard everything she said, even the silent thoughts she conveyed so clearly on her face. Blair wore her every emotion, and for some reason she was particularly easy for me to read. Though, she clearly didn't realize how attuned to her I was, or she'd know I'd heard her when she mentioned her love of kids, the college courses she was taking, and all the other details of her life that I clung to as though they were water and I was dying of thirst.

The elevator reached the lobby, and I silently cursed since it meant my time with Blair was over for the day. For the most part.

I gestured for her to walk off first, then kept in step with her as we exited the building into the crisp

October air. Before she could turn in the opposite direction as me, I put my hand on her shoulder and waited for her to meet my gaze.

I smiled softly and winked at her. "I'm sure you're perfect for the job." Blair's face flushed with red at my compliment, but she smiled brightly.

"Thanks, Mr—Justice." Then she spun around and trotted to the corner of Central Park West and disappeared around it, heading towards her Upper West Side private school. A soft wind blew, and it ruffled her sorry excuse for a skirt. I needed to do something about that. The thought of some horny teenage boy seeing what was mine had me on the verge of a homicidal rage. I took several deep breaths until I'd calmed down.

"See you later, bunny," I murmured before stalking over to my town car that had been idling a few feet away. I waved off Benjamin, my driver, when he began to exit the vehicle and opened my own door, then slid onto the back seat. He also served as my bodyguard, a necessary evil when you were worth more than a billion dollars.

With the tinted windows and dark interior, the ambiance matched my mood. I put the partition up so that I was alone and unzipped my pants, releasing my turgid cock. I placed a towel underneath my erection before laying my head back against the supple leather. I curled my hands around the edge of the seat and clenched them, holding on like I was afraid I'd be swept away in a tide. Then, like every day on the drive to Wall Street, I closed my eyes and allowed myself to indulge in my morning fantasy.

CHAPTER 2

JUSTICE

I caressed Blair's swollen belly as I kissed my way down to her naked pussy. I loathed the idea of anything between us, so I demanded that she keep it bare for me. There was nothing sexier than seeing her southern lips glistening with a mixture of her arousal and my seed.

My mouth watered as I leaned in and inhaled deeply, filling my lungs with the sweet and musky scent of her sex. I was addicted to eating her pussy, but for some reason, when she was pregnant, my obsession intensified and I craved it with a deep, gnawing hunger.

With one lick up her seam, Blair was already squirming and whimpering for release. I sucked lightly on her clit before dragging my tongue through her wetness again.

"Please, Justice," she begged. "I want you inside me."

I grinned against her pussy. My girl loved my cock and I was more than happy to oblige her, but I needed my taste first. "Patience, bunny," I crooned. Then I buried my face in her heat and licked and sucked, eating her and drinking down all her juices.

When she was pumping her hips up to meet my mouth and crying out my name, I latched onto her clit and plunged two fingers into her channel. With one swipe over her most sensitive spot, she came with a scream and a flood of her arousal filled my mouth.

"Fuck," I mumbled as I continued to lap at her and lazily pump my fingers. "I love it when you squirt your come down my throat."

I was pressing my pelvis hard into the mattress to try and relieve some of the pressure and keep from coming before I was balls-deep in her young pussy. Blair had learned to take me all the way like a champ. After one baby, you'd think she would loosen up, but she was still as tight and innocent as the day I popped her cherry. Just thinking about it made me want to roar like a fucking caveman.

I surged up between her legs, staying upright on

my knees so I wasn't leaning over and putting pressure on her round belly. Grabbing her ass, I elevated her so that I had the perfect angle to thrust in to the hilt. From this position, I had the perfect view of my cock disappearing into her pussy with the proof that I'd bred her right above.

The slight abrasions on her thighs from my whiskers and the sight of my cock coming out sticky and shiny from her come was enough to set me off right then. However, I managed to keep from completely blowing my load, though I was leaking a steady stream of come. "I swear you've gotten even tighter since I knocked you up, bunny," I grunted as I fought to draw my dick out of her so I could shove it back in. "You're squeezing the fuck out of my cock. Oh, fuck. Yes!"

I started slow, trying to draw it out. But as usual, once I got inside her, my body took over. "I can't hold back, baby," I gritted through clenched teeth. "I need you to come." Her pussy walls started to flutter then clench as shudders wracked her body. "Such a good girl," I praised, pressing on her clit to push her over the edge.

Blair began to chant, "Yes, yes, yes." Then she screamed as her orgasm crashed over her. "Justice!"

"Fuck!" I shouted. "Oh yeah, baby. Take it. Fuck,

yes!" Black spots filled my vision as I came with a vengeance, like being hit by a fucking freight train. Thick, strong jets of jizz spurted from my dick, filling her womb. I'd just had her a few hours ago to take care of my morning wood, but it seemed as though I had an endless supply of cream.

Eventually, my eyes cleared, and my erratic breathing slowed. I pulled out and grinned when Blair mewled in protest. "You still hungry for my cock, bunny?"

Her porn star lips turned down in an adorable pout, and she nodded. She looked so fucking beautiful with her long blonde hair wildly around her, her flushed skin, and her passion filled, blue eyes. My gaze drifted down to her large, milky tits. She was still nursing our first baby and drops of white liquid were beading on her nipples before dripping down the sides. She'd had a fantastic set before she got pregnant, but once she was knocked up, they'd grown to accommodate her supply of milk. I was almost as addicted to them as I was to her pussy.

Who was I kidding? I was obsessed with every part of Blair.

"Daddy needs his turn with your tits first," I told her; then I licked my lips in anticipation. Her arms had been spread out beside her, gripping the sheets, *but she moved them to her belly as she watched me with a heavy-lidded gaze. My cock had barely softened, and it immediately swelled to epic proportions when Blair slid her palms up to cup the heavy globes. She squeezed gently, causing more of her nectar to spill from the ripe mounds.*

I growled and quickly—carefully—rolled onto my back and put her astride me. She dropped down hard and fast, crying out when my tip hit her cervix. Grasping her hips, I sat up and took one succulent nipple into my mouth. I fed from her tits until I was satisfied, and she was riding me like I was a prized stud.

"Gently, bunny," I cautioned, worried about her being too rigorous while she was so far along.

"I can't help it," she panted as she rose up and dropped back down fast and hard.

Taking ahold of her lush, wide hips, I held her still and took over, pounding up into her pussy so I was doing all of the work.

Blair threw her head back and cried out in ecstasy as she splintered apart. I buried myself as deep as possible and latched onto one of her nipples again and bit. Not enough to really hurt, but enough to cause a spark of pain to mix with her pleasure. I knew it would intensify her orgasm, and I was rewarded with a deafening scream that echoed off the walls of our bedroom. Her pussy was wrapped so tightly around my cock that I couldn't have moved it if I wanted to.

I switched to the other nipple, and I detonated when her milk splashed into my mouth. The world ceased to exist as I came with such violence that I briefly wondered if I would survive. Who the fuck cared? I wouldn't want to go any other way.

My eyes popped open as the sound of my shout filled the back of the town car. Thankfully, the partition was soundproof, something I'd corrected after the first time I had my little fantasy.

I released my death grip on the bench seat and glanced down at my lap; grimacing at the sticky mess I'd made. Another lesson I learned after I'd ruined several pairs of pants. I stocked the car with hand towels when I realized I might as well give in to my morning day-dream because I always lost when I tried to fight it.

The crazy thing was, I hadn't even touched myself. Nobody else had either since I hadn't been interested in a woman since long before Blair. And I'd never needed to take myself in hand because my dick didn't have any reason to get hard. Then, once Blair became my obsession, I still didn't have the desire to take care of myself, despite sporting at least a semi pretty much all the time. It felt too much like betrayal. The only one who should be touching me, satisfying me, was my woman. And even in my dreams, she was able to do it.

I quickly cleaned up and threw the towel into a duffle bag I kept in the car for that exact reason. I dropped it at the cleaners on the weekends so that I was prepared again Monday morning.

The car slowed to a stop in front of my building just as I was tucking my somewhat limp dick back into my pants. I zipped up right before Benjamin opened my door. After a cursory glance to make sure no traces of my activities remained, I exited the vehicle.

At least I had my work, which I loved, to help keep my obsession from consuming my every thought throughout the day. Otherwise, I wasn't sure I'd have been able to stay away until the right time. There were so many days when I'd almost said fuck it and gave in to my need for her. But then logic would rear its ugly head and remind me that she'd be eighteen soon. I could wait.

CHAPTER 3

JUSTICE

"Thatcher's in your office," Patti, my secretary, announced when I reached her desk, situated just outside my door. I sighed—pretending I didn't already know why he was there—and speared her with a reproachful glare. "What the hell, Patti? What happened to being the gatekeeper?" Patti had been my secretary since my brother and I started our investment firm, K-Corp, fifteen years ago. She was in her early fifties now, had been married for over thirty years, and had three kids who were grown and lived in the city.

She'd been the first person to apply for the job, and my brother and I had instantly fought over who got to hire her as their assistant. Luckily, I won the coin toss. But she'd been more mother to both us than our own ever had been. Her husband and kids were family to us, too.

"Language, young man!" she snapped, pointing her pen at me.

I rolled my eyes since Patti could curse with the best of them. "Sorry, ma'am."

She nodded and patted her short, brown bob, brushing hair out of her face as she turned her attention to her computer screen.

"Um, Patti?"

"Hmmm?"

I put my hands on my hips and scowled. "Thatcher?"

"Oh yes, he's in your office," she repeated distractedly.

"Why?" I pressed.

"Because you're a selfish son-of-a-bitch and I have a fucking bone to pick with you." My brother stepped out of my office as he spoke, clearly fuming about something. Again, I pretended not to know why and simply raised a questioning brow.

"What he said," Patti added with a grin. Shit, she obviously knew why Thatcher was there too.

"Et tu, Patti?"

She just shrugged and started typing.

"I'm surrounded by crazy people," I grumbled

with a shake of my head as I brushed past Thatcher
into my office. "Enlighten me," I said to him as I took
a seat at my glass desk, my back to the spectacular
view of the Upper Bay and the Statue of Liberty.

"You seriously didn't expect me to put up a fight
when you foisted the Benson account on me?"

"Mr. Benson is one of our biggest clients,
Thatch"—I leaned back in my chair and looked him
straight in the eye—"He needs the best of the best,
and that's you."

Thatcher's gray eyes, so much like my own,
narrowed. "Don't bullshit me, bro. You just don't
want to deal with his vapid wife."

I shrugged and picked up a silver pen from the
desktop to fiddle with. "Maybe it's both."

"She's already sent me five texts this morning,
called twice, and emailed about setting up a 'private' appointment." He walked to my desk and
bent over so our faces were level. "I get why you
did it. I know you don't want her showing up in
the lobby and causing drama while Blair is in the
building." I glanced at the open door to my office,
then back to Thatcher frowning in warning. My
brother and I were only a year apart and had
always been close. We were best friends, and he
was the only one who knew about my obsession

with Blair. I wanted to keep it that way. He nodded in acknowledgment and lowered his voice. "But, pawning that succubus off on me?" Thatcher furrowed his brow and scowled. "You owe me big time, bro."

"I do," I agreed. My immediate capitulation seemed to un-bunch his panties, and the tension left his body.

He slumped down into one of the chairs across from me and put his feet up on my desk. "She starts today?"

I nodded, attempting to appear calm and unruffled, but the pen tapping a fast rhythm on the glass betrayed my agitated state.

Thatcher dropped his feet and sat forward, resting his elbows on his knees and steepling his fingers. His expression was dead serious. "You have to stay away," he said quietly.

Irrational anger streaked through me, but I managed to keep a damper on it. I opened the center drawer and tossed the pen inside with more force than was necessary. "I know."

U nable to resist another minute, I picked up my phone and swiped to open it. Then I found the app I was looking for and loaded it.

The daycare had several mounted cameras that allowed me to keep an eye on Blair while she was there. But, I'd worked out a curriculum with the instructor for her practicum that also required her to use a new app that was becoming standard in the industry. It was a real-time app that allowed the teachers to have instant access to medical history and other notes, as well as reminders and notifications from the parents. Parents could receive screenshots and video throughout the day, even using the app to request a photo or video update.

Blair had been given a phone—one I'd provided that allowed me to keep track of her location. Theo-retically, so that I would worry less about her safety. However, while it helped a little, I knew I wouldn't be satisfied until I was personally seeing to her safety.

The app was another tool to help me keep from doing something stupid. I'd made sure it came already installed and set up on her phone. Blair was instructed to use it throughout the day to keep a sort of video diary, especially while she was working in the daycare. I was sure she assumed the information was going to her professor, but I was the only one who had access to her app.

I was excited to see that she'd already uploaded a couple of videos, some notes, and screenshots. I went through them over and over until I had them memorized.

When my alarm went off at six, I closed the app and woke up the screen on my computer. After a few clicks, I was staring at the series of camera feeds in the daycare. They closed at six, so the last of the parents would be picking up their children.

Blair was standing by a window cradling a baby boy, no more than six months old, and swaying from side to side. She was cuddling him, once again reminding me of a sweet little bunny. She looked so natural and at ease. The expression on her face was practically blissful. I imagined it was a hint of the way she would look when I made her come.

A woman walked into the room and called to Blair, who turned around and smiled. If it were anyone but me, they might not have noticed that her smile was off. I leaned in and studied her more intently, anxious to know what was upsetting my girl.

The woman took the baby from Blair and kissed

him on the head. She smiled and said something to my bunny, then turned and walked towards the exit. My eyes remained glued to Blair. It was clear that she thought no one was looking because her mask had dropped away. Blair put her arms around herself, and her face was awash with pure longing as she watched the mother leave with her baby.

Soon, bunny. Soon.

hirty days. Thirty fucking days. I repeated this in my head over and over as I watched Blair reluctantly say goodbye to the babies in her care. Every fucking day of the week, I struggled to keep from running down to her and sweeping her away to take that look off her face.

I only had to endure 30 more days. Then I would be free to take her and give her what she obviously so desperately wanted.

Marriage and kids had never been in my plans until the day Blair became mine. Now, all I could think about was putting the ring burning a hole in my pocket on her finger and filling our penthouse with our little ones.

My eyes stayed glued to the monitors until Blair

had slung her purse over her chest and left the daycare. I hated that I couldn't keep watch over her when she wasn't in the building, but I was somewhat appeased by being able to track her phone.

Every day, she would leave after they closed at six and head home to the penthouse next to mine. Whenever possible, I timed it so I would bump into her in our building lobby so we could ride the elevator together. I knew I wasn't strong enough to give her a ride home. If we were alone in the back of my car, I wouldn't be able to withstand her irresistible mix of innocence and sexy and she'd never make it to her eighteenth birthday with her virgin cherry intact.

Instead, I followed her at a distance—something that annoyed Benjamin and made him ridiculously cranky—so that I was sure she was protected. When we were a block away, I flagged down my driver and we pulled up to the building just as she arrived.

Yeah, I was well aware of how fucking crazy I seemed. I could only imagine the field day a shrink would have with this level of obsession, but I honestly couldn't manage to muster up even one fuck to give.

Today was one of the rare days when I wasn't able to personally make sure she got home safely, and it made me grumpy as fuck. I sent Benjamin, who also happened to be former Italian Special Forces, to trail her and make sure she got home without incident. If he wondered at my odd actions concerning Blair, he never voiced it and I didn't offer an explanation.

Thatcher sauntered into my office, drawing my attention away from the app where I was staring at the little green dot representing my girl.

"Remind me why this meeting had to happen tonight?" I scowled.

"Jamison is getting married this weekend, and he'll be gone on his honeymoon for three months." Thatcher leaned against the doorway; his hands stuffed in his pockets. "We need this merger to go through before the fiscal year ends."

"Okay," I dragged out the word. "But why a dinner meeting? This couldn't have been done during lunch?"

Thatcher's gaze was on the wall of windows that made up the left side of my office, matching the one I sat in front of. He meandered over to look down the forty-five floors to the ground beneath us. "I'm not available for lunch meetings," he finally responded, his tone inattentive.

I stood and walked up beside him, staring in the

same direction, trying to discern what he was staring at. The Statue of Liberty? Battery Park, maybe? "Want to give me a little more explanation than that, brother?"

Thatcher cursed and turned away from the window. "She's there. Every day. It's the only time I have to see her."

My brow shot up, probably getting lost in my hairline. This was the first I was hearing of a "she."

"The one," he clarified before turning his dark, churning eyes on me.

I'd never known Thatcher to be anything less than completely confident. Seeing him unraveling at the seams told me how serious he was about this woman. "So, what's the problem? Why are you hesitating?"

He shook his head and pulled his hands from his pockets to cross his arms over his chest. "I'm not hesitating," he disagreed. "I'm just not ready yet. Everything has to be perfect."

"Everything?" I asked, still confused. Why hadn't he just gone and gotten his girl? "What are you waiting for?" The second Blair was legal, I was going to have her moved into our home and installed in our bed with her legs wide open so I could fuck my baby into her unprotected womb. And, I wouldn't let her leave until she'd made me a daddy. Possibly not even then...

Thatcher shook his head. "I'll explain another time. We're going to be late."

I decided to allow him to table the subject for now, but I'd be getting to the bottom of it later. I returned to my desk and grabbed my suit coat from the back of my chair, donning it. I gathered a stack of files for Patti and set them on her empty desk as we passed by. She'd gone home early for her daughter's birthday dinner. Another event I was missing due to this stupid meeting. Not that I would have gone. I knew I'd been a son-of-a-bitch lately and wasn't fit company.

I was surprised that Benjamin wasn't back yet, but I figured Blair must have stopped at the store on the way home. She cooked for her and her dad most nights. It was something she'd mentioned that she loved to do. Since my driver wasn't available, we grabbed a cab to the midtown steakhouse. I did my best to pay attention to the topic at hand and partici-pate in the conversation, but I kept glancing at my phone, waiting for a text from Benjamin telling me that Blair was home.

Finally, at around eight, I excused myself and

made my way outside. The phone only rang once before he picked up.

"What the fuck, B?" I nearly shouted.

"Calm down, Justice. She just got home. I'm headed in your direction."

"What was the holdup? It wouldn't have taken her this long just to go to the store."

"She went to a doctor's office in a building on Park before going to the store."

My whole body stiffened, and my heart leapt into my throat. "Doctor?" I croaked. Was something wrong with my girl?

"I don't think it's something to worry over," he assured me. "The only names listed on the directory were Gynecologists."

I let out the breath I hadn't realized I been holding. It was probably just her yearly checkup. Except...I frowned as I did the math in my head. No, she wasn't due for another three months.

"She did come out with a piece of paper clutched in her hand, though. And when she left the store, she had a pharmacy bag."

My eyes narrowed as his words sunk in, and the most likely scenario formed in my mind. A birth control prescription?

Over my dead fucking body.

"Get your ass here and get me home fast," I growled before hanging up. I shot a text to Thatcher, telling him I had an emergency and he could handle the meeting on his own. We had complete trust in each other, so I wasn't at all worried about leaving it in his hands.

Benjamin rolled to a stop in front of the restaurant and double parked so he could get out and open my door, using it as an excuse to do a visual sweep of the area. He shot me a frown, conveying his displeasure at my choice to dispatch him elsewhere and leave me unprotected.

He was in for a big surprise in a month when he found himself permanently on Blair's detail. Initially, I'd only intended to hire a bodyguard temporarily after some serious threats had been made towards Thatcher and myself while we were in the midst of a huge international deal. But, Benjamin and I had become friends and when I realized the role Blair was going to have in my life, I kept him on, knowing he would eventually be assigned to her. Though, I hadn't shared that plan with him yet.

I climbed into the car and lowered the partition as he got settled into the driver's seat. "I don't care what you have to do," I seethed. "Who you have to bribe, what the fuck ever. Make sure that doctor and all the others in her office refuse to write Blair another prescription."

Again, if Benjamin had questions about my demands, he kept them to himself. He simply nodded and tapped the screen in the dash to search his contacts. I rolled down the window next to me and stopped paying attention. I was lost in thought as I stared out into the dark night and enjoyed the spring breeze. I focused on the goal of getting rid of the birth control because if I thought about who she'd gone on it for, there was a good chance I would lose my mind.

I honestly had no idea what I was going to do when I got home, but I wouldn't rest until I was sure that Blair's body remained ripe and ready for me to breed.

As luck would have it, maybe it was a reward for my patience, Blair would be ovulating when she turned eighteen. I knew because in my fanatical need to know everything about her, I paid close attention. The day her backpack had spilled, a small side pocket had been partially unzipped and a few tampons had fallen out. From that day on, my eyes strayed to the pocket every morning, and I noticed that it was only full once a month.

"Taken care of, Justice." Benjamin's voice pulled

me from my thoughts, and I lifted my chin in acknowledgment when he glanced at me in the rearview mirror.

My building came into view, and I was out the door before the car had come to a complete stop. I raced inside and used my fob to unlock the penthouse elevator. I swore a blue streak at the slow ascent and vowed to call the maintenance company and order them to speed it up.

At long last, the car reached the top floor, and the doors whooshed open. My long stride ate up the distance to the door at the opposite end of the hall from mine, but I hesitated when I finally reached it.

The smell of something heavenly was seeping under the door and filling the hallway. My stomach growled, and I pictured the day when I would come home to smells like this coming from my own apartment. And the sight of my barefoot and pregnant wife in the kitchen. Which wouldn't happen as fast as I wanted if I didn't take care of those fucking pills.

I raised my hand and rapped on the door with my knuckles. Heavy footsteps got louder as someone approached the door. Probably Paul, Blair's father, since my girl walked with a light, graceful step. If I didn't know better, I would have thought she floated everywhere, like the angel she was.

After a few more steps, the lock disengaged, and the door swung open. However, it wasn't Paul greeting me from inside the apartment. It was a boy, a teenage punk in a school uniform with the same insignia as Blair's.

CHAPTER 5

JUSTICE

The little fucker had a cocky smirk on his pretty boy face, but it fell away the minute he clocked my expression. I imagined it looked as deadly as I felt.

"Uh, can I help you?" he stammered, though he tried to sound confident.

I ignored him and pushed inside. "Blair?" I called. Her apartment almost mirrored mine—though mine had a second floor—so I easily navigated straight to the kitchen. I almost fell to my knees at the vision in front of me. Blair's white-blonde hair was piled on top of her head, and she was wearing a white T-shirt and jean shorts that went to just above her knees. Thank fuck, I didn't think I could have handled anything else without my head exploding.

She had on a frilly pink apron and her feet were bare, showing off her cute, pink-tipped toes.

Something bubbled on the stove, and she stirred it until I rasped her name again. She jumped, clearly noticing me for the first time. Her cheeks bloomed with that pretty blush I loved so much.

"Where's your dad?" My tone was harsher than I meant for it to be from trying to control myself, and she took a step back. *Fuck fuck fuck.* I hated that I scared her. When I spoke again, I adopted a softer tone. "Is your dad here, bunny?"

I hadn't meant to let the nickname slip, but I enjoyed the slight widening of her eyes and the way the flush of her skin spread.

"He's in his office," she answered quietly.

I turned around and trained my gaze on the little shithead hovering behind me. "Leave." My tone brooked no argument, but the kid clearly had a death wish.

He puffed up his scrawny chest and gave me what I was sure was supposed to be a defiant glare, but just made him look like a pouting toddler. "Blair and I are working on a project."

"Out," I snapped.

He began to protest again but when I took a few menacing steps in his direction, backing him up into the living room, his mouth opened and closed like a fish. Then he caved and yelled, "I need to get going, Blair. We can work at my house next time."

I closed my eyes and pinched the bridge of my nose, willing myself to stay calm. I needed to remember that I couldn't take care of Blair from prison.

I stayed in that position until the front door clicked shut.

"Justice," I heard Blair snap from behind me. I spun around and almost smiled at how adorable she was. Her hands were on her hips, her face was scrunched in indignation, and her blue eyes were lit with fire. My bunny had more mettle than I thought. Why did that make me want her even more? "Our project is a huge portion of my grade, and I have a hard enough time getting him to work on it when we're together."

My eyes narrowed, and my hands clenched into fists. "What are you doing when you're supposed to be working?" Her answer was bound to piss me the fuck off, but I had to know.

Blair blushed and dug the toes of one foot into the thick carpet. "He mostly tries to convince me to go out with him," she sighed.

At that moment, I was more grateful than ever

that Blair was an open book to me. She was trying not to be negative, but I could see the annoyance in the downturn of her mouth.

"So, the birth control pills aren't for him?" I blurted. *Well shit. Nice going Justice.*

Blair's eyes became so big they almost swallowed her face, and she blushed so hard her skin was practically tomato red. "How did you...?"

"Answer the question," I cut her off; needing an answer.

Her eyes darted away, and she bit her bottom lip as she fidgeted, twisting her fingers around each other. "No."

"Who?" I prompted sternly.

"Nobody, I mean it was just in case..."

My gaze bored into hers, and she looked back at me with uncertainty. "In case?" I queried.

"I'm going to be eighteen at the end of the month," she explained hesitantly. "I thought maybe..." She was studying my face intently and for the first time, I couldn't discern what she was thinking from her expression or stance. It was unsettling, and I hated it. "Never mind," she said, her shoulders slumping.

Before I could say anything else, Paul strode into the room. "What's for dinner, sweet pea?" He stopped when he saw me and regarded me with confusion. "Justice. Did we have an appointment?" Paul was a great guy, but he was the epitome of the absent-minded professor. He was the dean over the school of music at The Juilliard School, but he came from family money, which was how he and Blair lived like they did. Despite his wealthy upbringing, he freely admitted that he had no clue how to manage his inheritance. I'd been handling his investments, working alongside his money manager, since I bought the building and moved into the penthouse across the hall. I didn't deal with smaller accounts anymore with only a few exceptions, Paul being one of them. I did it as much for Blair as my friendship with her father.

"No, Paul. I just needed to have a word with Blair. I wanted to offer my car and driver to get her from school to her internship and home."

Blair frowned but didn't have a chance to say anything before Paul smiled widely and nodded emphatically. "That's a generous offer, Justice. Normally, I wouldn't take you up on something bound to inconvenience you, but I do worry about my sweet pea coming home all the way from Wall Street in the evenings."

Blair rolled her eyes. "I've been getting around

this city by myself since I was ten, Daddy. I don't think—" I cut her a warning look, and she shut her mouth.

"Still, can't be too careful." Paul walked over to Blair and wrapped his arm around her shoulder, then kissed her temple. After a moment, his eyes shifted back in my direction. "You're welcome to stay for dinner."

"I'm sure he's far too busy," Blair interjected. My stomach chose that moment to emit another hungry rumble.

Paul laughed uproariously and beckoned me in their direction before turning towards the dining room. "I'm sure a bachelor like you rarely has a home cooked meal, and my Blair is a whiz in the kitchen. I don't know how I'd survive without her."

I clamped my jaw together to keep from informing him that he would need to solve that mystery by the end of the month or starve.

"I'll set another place," Blair murmured before disappearing into the kitchen.

There was something I had to do before I could relax and enjoy the meal. I glanced at the kitchen; then gave Paul an innocent smile and cocked my head towards the hallway. "I'm just going to use the restroom."

He mirrored the tilt of my lips and waved in the same direction I'd indicated. "I'm sure you know where it is," he laughed. I nodded and spun on my heel, marching down the hall with purpose. The apartment had three bedrooms, and I guessed right when I pushed open the door to the first one on the right.

The room was decorated in white and lavender with yellow accents; it was feminine without being overkill. Everything was in its place except the stack of worn paperbacks on the nightstand that had me chuckling. Blair had always been a bookworm. It was one of the few things I remembered about her as a child and something we had in common. A grin sliced across my face when I pictured her reaction to one of the improvements I'd made to my home when I moved in.

I knew I didn't have much time before my bathroom excuse became awkward, so I did a quick sweep of the room and decided that the most likely place was the white-washed, antique vanity on the wall by a door that I knew led to an ensuite bathroom. After a thorough examination of the drawers, I came up empty, so I moved on to the washroom.

Figuring it was the most obvious choice, I opened the mirrored door to the medicine cabinet first. A little, round, blue container caught my attention first, and I took it from the shelf. I opened it to find a packet of white pills and grunted in approval when I didn't find any of them missing. It wasn't like I would have had her stomach pumped or anything, but I was still happy not to have to worry about even one pill.

I started popping them out into my palm, one by one. "Justice! What are you doing?" Blair gasped as she rushed into the bathroom and tried to make a grab for the container. I held it above her head, which was easily done considering our height difference, and finished emptying the packet.

I tossed the container into the trash can and stalked over to the small room that contained the toilet. Glancing in Blair's direction, I made sure she was watching when I lifted the lid and tossed the offending pills in and flushed.

She stood in silent shock and just stared at me as I prowled over to her. When I got into her space, she backed up. But I followed, and soon I had her trapped between me and the wall.

"Why did you do that?" she asked in a raspy tone. Her eyes looked suspiciously watery as they locked with mine, and I wanted nothing more than to kiss her and make it better.

"You don't need them," I stated.

"How would you know?" she snipped. Her attempt to be confident was ruined by the pretty shade of pink suddenly dusting over her cheeks and nose.

I leaned down until our lips were only a whisper apart. "Because I can smell that innocent little cherry from here, bunny."

Her mouth formed a little O, and she sucked in a breath. "Um...well, I was hoping to—um—you know —" she stammered, her blush intensifying as she broke eye contact. "Maybe I don't want to be a virgin anymore," she uttered suddenly, then slapped a hand over her mouth.

Blair's eyelids dropped, and she looked shyly up at me through her lashes. "I guess I was hoping the guy I want would want me too." Her voice was soft as a whisper, and her warm breath bathed my lips, making me crave their touch.

"They don't want *you*," I growled thinking about those pricks who only wanted in her panties and weren't interested in the real her, in treating her like she deserved.

Her expression crumbled, and she shrunk into the wall. "Okay. I guess you're right then. I don't need the birth control. Clearly, I won't be having sex if nobody wants me."

My head reared back in disbelief. What the fuck? Then it hit me, how what I said could be misconstrued. "I meant those boys only want one thing from you, bunny," I explained. "They don't want the real you, all of you." I didn't bother to disguise the longing in my voice. "Besides, those little shits wouldn't know the first thing about pleasuring a woman."

"Do you?" Blair asked softly.

My head dipped, and I closed the distance between our faces again. "Do I what?"

"Know what to do in—um—bed?"

A wicked smile curved my lips, and I traced my lips along her cheek, so light they were barely touching, until I reached her ear. "I know how to please *my* woman."

Blair's breathing picked up, and we were so close that her big tits rubbed against my chest. When I felt her hard nipples, I groaned and dropped my face into the crook of her neck. "Thirty days," I rumbled.

"What?" Blair panted.

I slid my hands to her ass and yanked her forward so she could feel every inch of my hard cock pressing into the heat of her pussy. "Thirty fucking days, bunny."

Her hands grasped my biceps, and she gripped

them tightly, her nails digging into my skin through my dress shirt. "What's in thirty days?"

One of the threads holding me together snapped, and I gave in to a desperate urge. I brought my head back in position and pressed my mouth to hers. Electricity zinged straight to my dick and sparks flew. One second before I lost it, I forced myself to pull away rather than following my instincts and deepening the kiss.

"In thirty days. You're mine."

CHAPTER 6

May thirty-first was officially my favorite day of the year. It was the day Blair graced this world with her glowing presence. It was the day my bunny turned eighteen. And, it was the day she would officially be mine. Fina-fucking-ly.

"You're quite the contradiction today," Patti chirped as she traipsed into my office.

I raised a brow and leaned back in my chair, the fingers of my left hand playing aimlessly with my silver pen. "Contradiction?"

She nodded and set a stack of folders in front of me. "Sign and return to me," she instructed. Then she took a seat in one of the deep, leather chairs in front of me. "If you didn't have that permanent smile plastered on your face, I'd say you were downright grouchy."

"I'm confused," I admitted with a chuckle.

Patti eyed me for a few moments then relaxed in the chair and crossed one leg over the other. "I'm guessing it's impatience." Her tone was calculating, and her probing stare made me squirm in my seat. "Today's the day, isn't it?"

"Pardon?" I watched her warily, wondering what she thought she knew. She couldn't possibly...right?

"She turns eighteen today?"

I gaped at her in silence.

"When are you boys going to realize that I know everything?" she asked smugly.

I laughed and shook my head because she was absolutely right. I didn't know why I deluded myself into thinking she didn't know what was going on.

There was nothing that would stop me from fulfilling my plans, but Patti's opinion did mean a lot to me. It was why I'd hidden my feelings for Blair from her. I was afraid she would tell me that I was too over the top, that my obsession with Blair was unhealthy. That said, it wouldn't stop me, but her disapproval would sting.

"Yes, today is her birthday," I confirmed.

Patti was quiet for a minute, watching me with

an unreadable expression. Then she smirked. "You remind me of Don." Don was her husband, and it was a huge compliment to be compared to the man she adored. "I never told you how we met, or what our courtship was like because I wasn't sure how you boys would take it."

I almost blanched at the tiny bit of nervousness in her tone. But I managed to keep my expression neutral. She was nervous about our approval? My chest warmed at the thought that she wanted our respect as much as we wanted hers.

"You'll have to get Don to tell you his side of the story. I'm sure it's very different from mine," she tittered. "My version is that he came, he saw, he kidnapped."

Well shit. I was hooked. I stopped playing with my pen and leaned on the desk to listen intently.

"Don was an intern at my father's firm. They're both architects. Anyway, he saw me bring my dad lunch one day and according to him, he fell for me right that moment. He asked my dad about me, and my father thought I was too young for Don. I had just barely turned eighteen, and Don was fifteen years older than me. So Dad wouldn't give him any information about me or a way to contact me."

Patti's complexion pinkened as she continued,

and I was hanging on her every word. "The next time I showed up with lunch, Don was ready. Apparently, he'd been focused on nothing but me for weeks. He caught me at the elevator and dragged me into an empty office." She cleared her throat and sat up primly in her seat. "We'll skip over that; it was the boring part of the story anyway." Her blush and sly smile said otherwise, but I stayed quiet so she would continue. "Fast forward from there and the next thing I knew, I was in Don's car and we were driving to a house he'd rented on the beach in Connecticut."

Patti held out her hand and admired the diamond and gold wedding set on her hand with a soft smile. "He had me running down the aisle less than a week later. Much to my father's frustration. But, after he saw the way Don loved me, he came around fast."

Her point didn't escape me. "You think Blair's dad will come around?" I asked. It was something else that had bothered me, but since it wouldn't change my decision, I hadn't dwelt on it. Still, I wanted my girl to be happy, and it would be hard if her dad wasn't supportive of our relationship.

Patti stood and leaned across my desk to pinch my cheek. I rolled my eyes but took her hand and kissed the back before she took it back. "Don't tell

Don I did that," I hurried to say. I may not have known that whole story, but Don's possessiveness and jealousy when it came to Patti was no secret.

"I know you, Justice. If you didn't love this girl with all that you are, you wouldn't be interested at all." She straightened back up and padded over to the door, then paused and looked back at me. "Just be you and love her with everything you've got. What other people think isn't important. Blair is the only one that matters. If you love her like she deserves, if you put her first, her dad will come around."

She stepped through the door but popped her head back in when I called her name. "Thanks." She smiled brightly and nodded. "Now, go get your girl and stop being such an ass around here. Two years is long enough to deal with your Oscar the Grouch routine."

I laughed heartily as she disappeared then followed her instructions, quickly finishing up with a few emails and signing the documents Patti had given me. I handed them to her as I passed her desk. "Take the rest of the day off," I told her. "Actually, you might as well take next week off. I doubt I'll be here."

Patti chuckled and waved me off. "If I'm not

here, this place would fall apart." She wasn't wrong. "But I might leave a little early every day. Now go," she encouraged with a shooing motion.

I grinned and gave her a smart salute before striding to the elevator and taking it to the first floor where the daycare was located. The wait was finally over.

CHAPTER 7

W hen I walked into the daycare, Pandora, the manager, was sitting at the front desk doing paperwork. She looked up with a warm smile, but it turned puzzled when she saw me. "Um, Mr. Kendall, is there something I can do for you?"

I nodded and lifted my chin in the direction of the classrooms. "I'm here for Blair."

Her mouth turned down in a confused frown. "I don't understand, is there a problem? Because she's been doing a fantastic job. She's a natural with the kids."

That put a smile on my face. Yes, my girl was going to be an amazing mother. "There's no problem," I reassured her. "It's her birthday, and we're going to celebrate."

"Oh, okay." She sounded relieved, and I cocked my head to the side curiously. "I was worried that you were pulling her internship or something." She smiled sheepishly and shrugged. "Honestly, when you told me to hire her, I was skeptical. But now, I really don't know how we could live without her."

"You're the reason they hired me?" We both turned at the sound of Blair's voice. She was standing at the entrance of one of the classrooms, holding an infant in her arms. My dick practically wept at the sight. "Why would they do that just because you asked them to?" she asked, clearly perplexed.

"Mr. Kendall is the boss, Blair," Pandora said with a chuckle. "When he says jump, we say 'how high?'"

Blair's clear blue eyes turned to study me, and I wanted to smack myself upside the head for being so dumb. I'd forgotten that she didn't know I owned the company she worked for or that I'd created her "internship." This wasn't how I'd envisioned her finding out, but that's where we were.

"I created the position, but you were absolutely qualified for it," I told her, holding my hands out to the sides; palms up.

"K-Corp," she said slowly, putting emphasis on the K. "Justice Kendall." She shook her head and closed her eyes, her cheeks turning pink. "I can't believe I never put that together."

I covered the distance between us in two strides and glided my fingertips over her cheeks, then along her jaw. "I wasn't exactly up front about it," I acknowledged softly.

When her eyes opened again, she peered up at me through her lashes, and a bright smile stretched across her face. "I can't believe you did that for me." Her blush deepened, but she lifted her head fully to meet my gaze. "You remembered that I wanted to work with kids?" Her tone was filled with wonder, and I smiled tenderly.

"You'd be surprised how much I remember," I teased with a wink. She blushed, and I shifted my stance to hopefully hide my raging hard on. "As incredible as you look with that baby in your arms, let Pandora take her and go get your things."

Blair's expression clouded with confusion and a little fear. "Are you ending my internship?"

"Absolutely not," I denied with a shake of my head. "But you're done for tonight." My eyes drifted to Pandora, and I cocked my head towards Blair. The manager hurried over and scooped the baby from Blair's arms.

Once again, that same longing lingered in her eyes as she watched them walk away.

"Patience, bunny," I murmured; then nearly groaned at the memories of saying that to her in my fantasies. We needed to get the fuck out of there so I could sink into her barely legal pussy and give her the baby she so desperately wanted. "Go get your backpack, Blair. We're leaving."

"I'm leaving with you?" She was clearly perplexed by what was happening, but now wasn't the time to explain it in detail so I just nodded. "Where are we going?" she asked.

"To celebrate your birthday." It was the absolute truth. We were going to celebrate with a special dinner at home, and then I was going to commemorate the day she became mine by popping her teenage cherry. "Hurry, bunny." I encouraged her by turning her around and giving her a pat on her deliciously rounded ass.

She glanced back at me over her shoulder. Her eyes were round with shock, but she was silent as she ducked into the classroom. A minute later, she was back at my side with her backpack slung over one shoulder, and I immediately took it from her. Blair looked up at me through her lashes and smiled sweetly. "Thank you."

I returned her smile and gave her long ponytail a playful tug. "Anything for my girl." She looked like she wanted to say something, even opened her mouth but shut it after a beat. "Let's go." I held the front door of the daycare open and gestured for her to walk in front of me. My intentions were chivalrous, but I didn't waste the opportunity to watch her wide hips and perfect ass sway as she sashayed through the lobby and out of the building.

Benjamin was waiting at the curb, lounging against the black limousine and scanning his surroundings. When he spotted us, his eyes swept over Blair, making me clench my jaw and remind myself that I'd scare Blair if I beat the shit out of him in front of her. I was also grateful that she had changed out of her school uniform. While it was sexy as hell and I had every intention of fucking her in it, I didn't like anyone else seeing her that way. The day she graduated would be the last time she wore it in front of anyone but me.

Benjamin grinned and gave me a chin lift before opening the back door. I glared at him when he moved to help her into the car, and he backed off with a smirk. Once she was inside and out of earshot,

I leaned close and threatened in a low tone, "Eyes to yourself B and lose the smirk before I permanently disfigure that pretty-boy face of yours." Benjamin smoothed out his expression, but his eyes still danced with laughter.

Choosing to ignore him, I slid onto the black leather bench seat, and he shut the door behind me. I blinked a few times to let my eyes adjust to the darkened interior, but I didn't have to see Blair to know she was only a few inches away.

I dropped my head back and closed my eyes, trying to relax for a minute as the car glided into traffic. If I didn't get myself under control, I was going to end up with her riding my dick the whole way home. As appealing as the idea was, I refused to take Blair for the first time in the back of a car. Besides, the rug burns from fucking her on the floor would sting like a bitch.

"Justice?"

Her sweet voice warmed me all over, and the sound of my name falling from her perfect mouth caused a smile to crease my face. I opened my eyes and turned my head to gaze at her. Her hands were fidgeting in her lap, and I stilled them by covering them with one of my own. "Yes?"

My attitude must have eased some of her anxiety

because she returned my smile and the tension left her hands. "Where are we going?"

"Home, bunny. We're going home."

She canted her head, and her cute little nose scrunched as she thought about my answer. "But you said we were going to celebrate."

Unable to stand the distance any longer, I cupped her hips and dragged her over until she was sitting astride me. Even in the darkness of the car, I could see her flush as she bit her bottom lip. There was some shyness to her reaction, but I was more interested in the heat sparking in her baby blues. Gently, I pried her lip free before giving in to one of my fantasies and taking it between my own teeth.

Blair gasped, and her hands flew from her lap to clutch my biceps. I nibbled on her lip, then licked the velvety brim to soothe the sting. She moaned, and my cock jumped, startling her when she felt the movement beneath her.

"We are, bunny. We're just going to do it at home," I clarified softly. My lips roved over her silky skin, nibbling and kissing all along her jaw and down her neck. "Our home."

She gasped and started to tremble as her grip on my arms tightened. I swiftly raised my head to search her face and almost let out an audible sigh when I saw only hope shining in her blue pools.

"Our?" she echoed.

I nodded, and my hands traveled around until I was palming her ass. Then I jerked her forward so that her pussy was plastered against the straining bulge in my slacks. "I told you that in thirty days you would be mine." The words were raspy from the effort it was taking to keep from coming. I didn't want to waste a single drop of my sperm. Until she was carrying our baby, I was only going to come inside her.

Once that mission was completed, then I'd start on all of my other fantasies. I was going to fuck her tits before coming all over them. Then I was going to put her on her knees and teach her how to suck my dick deep in her throat before swallowing everything I had to give her.

I groaned and shouted at myself in my head to get my shit together. Today was not the day to let my little head rule me.

Blair had practically melted into me, and I buried my face in the crook of her neck. "All mine, bunny." My tongue darted out for a tiny lick, and I bit back a moan at her fruity taste. I was suddenly starving and wanted to feast by licking every inch of her skin

"Why, um, why do you call me bunny?"

I smiled against her skin and gave her a swift kiss on her collarbone before straightening my back so I could gaze down into her beautiful face. "Because you're so sweet and shy," I told her with a lopsided smile. "I'm betting you're a cuddler, too." Blair giggled and ducked her head, but not before I saw her lips tip up and pink dust her cheeks.

I placed a long finger under her chin and tilted her head back so I could see her entire face. "There's another reason why bunny so naturally fit you in my mind." It had been a fleeting thought the first time I called her that in my head, but it lurked in the back of my mind whenever I used her nickname.

Blair stared at me, waiting for me to elucidate and part of me wanted to kiss her while I did it. The other, stronger part, wanted to watch her face as I told her, "Because we're going to fuck like bunnies until you're breeding."

CHAPTER 8

Heat and excitement flared in Blair's eyes as she stared at me with an open mouth, and I suppressed a triumphant grin. I waited for her to digest my announcement and after a minute, she squeaked, "You want to get me pregnant?" I hadn't considered how fucking sexy it would be to hear her say that. My cock was so swollen that I wasn't sure how much longer my zipper would be able to contain it.

My hands drifted up her back, and I jerked my head from side to side once. "I *am going* to get you pregnant, little bunny."

Before either of us could say another word, we were startled by a sharp rap on the window. A quick glance to my right revealed that we'd arrived at our building. I'd been so wrapped up in Blair that I hadn't noticed the car slowing and coming to a complete stop.

I kissed Blair on the forehead, then grasped her waist and lifted her off of my lap. With one knuckle, I tapped the glass to let Benjamin know we were ready. My other hand wrapped firmly around one of Blair's.

The door opened and I scooted out, then helped Blair alight next to me. Benjamin kept his eyes averted and I grunted in approval, glad to see that he'd taken me seriously.

"I've set up interviews for you tomorrow," I informed him. "I'll let you handle finding your replacement." He nodded and I gave him a small wave, my mind already somewhere else.

My legs were much longer than Blair's, and I was in a huge fucking hurry. To avoid forcing her to run to keep up, I just swept her up into my arms and strode into our building.

On the elevator ride up to the penthouse floor, Blair asked me if I was firing Benjamin. I explained to her that he was hiring me a new security detail because she was now his top priority. I focused hard on the conversation because it was the only thing keeping me from taking her up against the wall.

Though it was definitely on the "to do" list for another time.

It wasn't until we were finally inside our apartment with the door shut and locked that I realized the weight I'd been carrying around. While my shoulders felt ten times lighter, my damn cock felt ten times heavier. I needed to get inside her before I nutted in my pants.

The dining room was set up for a birthday party, complete with streamers, balloons, and a shit ton of presents. I'd had every intention of waiting until after dinner, cake, and presents, but reality smacked me in the face and I walked right past, headed straight for our bedroom.

"I promise we'll have a party later, bunny," I told her with only a trace of regret. "I can't wait another minute to see this body I've been fantasizing about for so long. And if I'm going to knock you up tonight, I should probably get an early start." I set her down beside the bed and cupped her face tenderly in my hands. She wore a glazed expression, passion-filled and hungry.

I swallowed hard as I did something I'd been dreaming of for years. Cradling the back of her skull with one hand, I used the other to draw the rubber band down her hair and tossed it aside. I'd never seen her wear her hair down. Staring at it now, floating around her shoulders and tumbling down her back, I was filled with relief that she always wore it up. If any other man ever saw her like this, they'd fight me to the death for this stunning creature.

My eyes moved on to roam over her facial features, admiring her beauty for a few beats before I lowered my head. Our lips touched and when I licked the seam and she immediately opened for me, the world seemed to shift under my feet. Everything came together in complete harmony. Our first kiss was more than I could even imagine. Sparks flew and fire raced from my mouth straight to my dick. She tasted like peaches, and I couldn't get enough.

"I'll be gentle, Blair," I promised in a raspy voice. "But I've waited so long, this first time is going to be fast." She moaned in response, and I wasn't sure if she even really comprehended what I was saying.

Not more than a few minutes later, I had us both stripped and Blair laid out on the center of our bed. "Your curves are even more mouthwatering that I realized," I grunted as I took a moment to admire her form. I straddled her thighs and cupped her full-sized tits. "These are perfect for nursing babies. And, giant enough to feed me too." I couldn't wait to taste her sweet nipple juice.

Bending down, I sucked on each of her large nipples in turn. Blair's hands dove into her hair, clenching the strands as she wiggled and moaned from my ministrations.

Next, I latched onto her hips and leaned down to place a kiss on each one. "Wide and open, made for taking me deep and carrying our babies. Fuck, bunny," I breathed reverently. "Your body was created for baby-making." I moved back until I was kneeling between her knees and ran my palms up her legs. I stopped when I reached her thick thighs and licked my lips as I stared at her bare, glistening pussy. "I'm going to have you lasered so there will never be anything between us," I told her as I petted her mound. She squirmed, and I dipped a finger between her folds and ran it over her clit before slowly pushing it inside her virgin hole.

"Fuck!" I cursed as I worked the digit in. She was so fucking snug that I had no doubt the squeeze would be a little painful on my dick, but it would be completely worth it. And, it meant her pussy would milk it and suck up every drop of my seed.

"You want a baby, don't you, Blair?" I purred as I moved my finger in and out. She moaned and nodded, her legs instinctively spreading farther apart. "I know you do. I've watched you every day, and I saw how you looked at those babies, bunny. It's all you've ever wanted, isn't it? To be a mommy?"

Blair's eyes widened just a fraction, showing her surprise at either my stalking or my perceptiveness. I wasn't sure which. But when her inner walls clamped down on my finger, I took it as a sign that she wanted me to continue.

"Don't worry, bunny. I'm going to give you what you want. What we both want." I slipped a second finger in and stretched her muscles, getting her ready to take my fat cock. "Once I pop your cherry, I'm going to fuck you until I've given you all of my come. Then, when you've had time to rest, I'm going to mount you like a fucking animal until you've made me a daddy."

Blair whimpered, and her pelvis bucked up to meet my finger thrusts. I knew she'd be softer and more open if she came first, so I scooted down onto my belly and shoved my face in her sex. My mouth licked and bit at her clit while my hand pumped. My whiskers brushing over her soft skin only seemed to drive her even more crazy. When she was writhing and crying out my name, right on the edge, I drew my fingers out. She started to whine in protest, but it became a keening wail when I replaced my fingers with my stiffened tongue and speared in and out of her channel as I plucked her little pleasure button like the strings of a violin. Her flavor burst on my tongue, and I wondered if I was turning blue from the effort not to come. My balls probably looked like giant blueberries.

Blair's whole body froze for a beat, even her breathing had stalled. Then she threw back her head and screamed as she came with a series of violent shudders.

While her body was pulsing with her orgasm, I pushed back up onto my knees and pressed Blair's legs as wide as they would go. I lined up my cock with her entrance, then stopped as a thought came to me.

My hand darted out and I grasped her chin tightly, forcing her to look at me. "Did you stay off the pill like I told you to?" I demanded. She swallowed hard as she tried to focus on my words, but she was struggling since she was basically mid-orgasm. "Did you keep your body pure and ripe for me, Blair?"

She finally managed a nod, and I smiled as I caressed her face. "Good girl, bunny. You're ovulating so your body is primed and ready, just begging to be filled. There's nothing stopping me from putting my baby inside your soft belly." I snatched a pillow from the top of the bed and slid it under her hips.

I leaned forward and took hold of her wrists, pulling her hands from her hair and bring them down to her pussy. "Hold it open for me, baby," I instructed her. Her cheeks reddened through the pink flush of her heated skin, but she did as she was told. She used the fingers of each hand to open her folds, baring her soaked, pink flesh. Her clit was swollen and hard, making it pop out of its hood.

I watched intently as I slipped the engorged tip of my cock in her tight heat and then groaned at the snug fit. I gritted my teeth in an effort to be gentle as I sunk in a little more until I hit her innocence.

"Knowing that this pussy is untouched and I'm the only man who will ever feel its blissful grip is hot as fuck," I growled as I broke through Blair's barrier with one hard thrust. I gave her a little time to adjust to my size, but her shudders had subsided, and her heart rate was quickly decelerating. I wanted to come in her while her cervix was soft, so I started to move as soon as I felt she could handle it.

"Justice," she moaned.

It was like throwing gasoline on a blazing inferno. "Say it again," I snarled as I picked up my pace, practically pounding her into the mattress.

"Justice."

"Fuck, I love hearing you say my name while I'm rutting inside your pussy."

I was getting too close and needed to make sure she came again when I blew so that her womb was open. Sliding my hands under her ass, I lifted her up so I could go deeper and hit her clit with every pass. "Fuck!" I shouted when her walls clamped down hard. It hurt like hell, but the pain heightened my ecstasy and caused me to go off like a fucking rocket. I shoved in as far as I could go until my dick hit her cervix, and her pussy lips wrapped tight around it.

Blair's body froze, strung tight for a couple of seconds before she screamed and shattered. Her pussy convulsed around my cock as she came, sucking me dry. "Such a good little girl," I crooned as I rocked into her, the small movement enough to draw out her orgasm but not enough to actually break the seal.

I wanted nothing more than to clamp my legs around hers, roll to my back, and fall asleep buried in my baby girl's pussy. But judging from how tight she was, I knew it would cause her to be sore longer and I wanted her to heal as quickly as possible. I hated the thought of her hurting...and I couldn't wait to get back to making babies.

Slowly, I withdrew and though she clenched her legs to keep me from leaving, she also whimpered in pain. "Let me take care of you, bunny."

I climbed off the bed and jogged to the master bath, my dick bouncing because while I'd softened just a touch, I was still fully erect. A stack of washcloths sat folded on a shelf in between the double sinks. I lifted the top one off the pile and ran it under warm water.

My cock was covered in her sweet cream and it had a pink tinge to it, proof that I'd made her a woman. I hesitated to wipe it off, wanting to wear the proof like a badge of honor. However, I was afraid Blair might realize just how bat-shit-crazy I was if she saw me coveting her virgin blood. I needed to make sure she was madly in love with me, wearing my ring, and carrying our baby before she saw the true extent of my obsession with her. Otherwise, it might send her running. Not that she'd get far. I wasn't ever going to let her go. If she got freaked, she'd come around eventually.

After cleaning myself up, I took a fresh, wet cloth back to the bed and tenderly washed between her legs. "You're pretty red, bunny," I sighed. "Shit. I shouldn't have taken you so hard your first time."

Blair drew my attention by placing a hand on my

arm. "It was perfect," she whispered when our eyes met. There was nothing but sincerity in her blue depths.

"I'm happy you feel that way." Our lips met in a sweet kiss, then I pressed her back down onto the bed. I made sure she was still situated with the pillow angling her hips up, then crawled in and laid down beside her. I put one arm under her head and cupped one of her ample tits with my free hand, then threw one leg over both of hers. "It just means I'll have to get creative for the next day or so," I murmured sleepily.

"Creative?" she sounded amused, and it brought a smile to my lips.

"Creative ways to fill your pussy with my come without hurting you," I explained. Then my tone turned cocky. "Don't worry, I have endless ideas when it comes to your body, bunny."

CHAPTER 9

JUSTICE

When I woke from our nap, Blair was awake and studying me with a worried expression while she chewed on her bottom lip.

"Don't, Blair," I admonished. "I'm the only one who gets to bite that lip." Yep. I was jealous of fucking teeth.

I brushed loose strands of straight blonde hair back from her face. "What's going on in that head of yours, bunny?"

"What is this?" she asked timidly.

"This?" I raised a brow. "You're going to need to be a little more specific. And I'm going to assume you aren't talking about my dick because that would just be insulting."

Blair giggled, but the smile didn't quite reach her eyes. "I meant, this—you know—us."

I leaned up on my elbow so I could see all of her face while we talked. "That's it. Us."

She looked confused by my answer.

"You"—I pointed at her chest—"me"—I pointed at my own chest and then at her tummy—"and baby makes three. For now."

Blair laughed, and the beautiful bell-like sound warmed my heart and hardened my cock. "So, I'm your baby momma?" She asked it flippantly, but as usual, she wore her true feelings on her face, and I could clearly see that she was afraid I was going to say yes.

"Bunny." I turned her on her side so we were facing each other. "Don't ever refer to yourself like that again. You are the mother of my children—"

"As in plural?" she interrupted with a squeak. Her face flushed with delight, clearly liking the idea.

"I intend to keep you pregnant for a long time," I stated. "You're going to be too irresistible when you're wearing my ring and dripping milk from your sexy tits." I licked my lips in anticipation as I eyed her chest hungrily.

"Justice?"

"I fucking love the way you say my name," I sighed.

"Justice, focus!" she snapped.

My head flew up in surprise, and I grinned at the glimpse of her backbone. I loved that my girl was so soft and sweet, but I had a feeling that attitude I glimpsed from time to time would end up making her a tigress in bed.

"What, bunny?"

"Did you say ring?"

I frowned. "Of course, I said ring. You think I'd let my wife walk around without a ring, so every bastard around her knows she's taken?"

Blair tensed and stared at me in silence.

"What?" I finally asked.

She huffed with impatience, and it was cute as fuck.

"Are you going to ask me?"

"Ask you what?"

"To marry you!" she practically shouted.

My brows drew down, and I scowled. "Absolutely not."

Blair sat up and stared down at me incredulously. "You just said you wanted me to have your babies and wear a ring. But we're not getting married?"

I shifted so I was sitting up too before replying. "We are getting married." My tone made it clear this was not up for debate.

Blair shouted in frustration and pulled on her hair. "What the heck are you talking about? How can we get married if you aren't asking me?"

Ah, then it all made sense. "Bunny, I'm not asking because you have no other choice. We're getting married, and that's final."

"So...." She started ticking off her fingers as she made a list. "I'm moving in"—I nodded—"we're getting married"—another nod—"and I'm apparently going to be baring you a gaggle of babies. Does that about sum it up?"

Her voice held a hint of sarcasm, and I narrowed my eyes while I waited for her to make her point.

"Why? Why do you want all that with me?"

"Because I love you," I said with exasperation.

"Oh."

I laughed at her befuddled expression. She clearly hadn't expected my answer. Although I didn't know how she hadn't figured that out yet. "Bunny, I've loved you since long before I should have." I decided to lay it all out for her. "There are no limits to my obsession with you, Blair. I'm going to be a possessive, jealous, domineering asshole sometimes, but no one will ever love you more than I do."

She clasped her hands in front of her chest, and I was very proud of the fact that I didn't let it draw my eyes down to her tits. "I love you, too," she chirped brightly.

"Good." I gently pushed her shoulder until she was once again lying on her back. "Now, let's work on those babies." After adjusting the pillow, I decided to eat her pussy until she came, then come all over it and push as much of it as I could inside. After that, I jacked off with my dick inside only an inch or so. Then we fell into another exhausted heap and slept.

It was morning when we woke up next. Actually, she woke me when she dragged me out of bed, having discovered the birthday set up she hadn't noticed the night before.

She opened her presents, the last one being a little blue box that contained a five-carat diamond ring that I slipped on her third, left finger.

While she went into the bedroom to put her new things away, I made my way to the kitchen and served up a huge slice of her cake. When I walked back into the bedroom, she was looking around with a puzzled and slightly amused expression.

She was clearly just noticing that all of her things were already moved in and put away. Talking her dad around to my way of thinking had taken work even though she was going to be right next door, but he'd finally caved when he realized I wasn't going to budge. But, that was all forgotten when she spotted the plate in my hand. Her eyes lit up like a kid on Christmas morning.

I swaggered over to her, and she reached for it but I held it away. "You can have some cake, but I'm going to feed it to you."

She opened her mouth, and I smirked. "Nope. We're going to eat it my way."

She quickly learned that my way meant I fed her some cake and ate the rest off of her body. After licking most of the frosting from her pussy, I buried my eleven inches to the hilt and filled her like a Twinkie with my own thick, sticky cream.

Almost 2 years later...

Sweet milk splashed in my mouth as my orgasm barreled through me. I sucked hard on her nipple, hungry for more as my hips punched up while my wife rode my cock and cried out my name. "Gently, bunny," I cautioned her as I stroked her swollen belly.

Sucking Blair's milky tits while I fucked her always made me come so hard, I nearly passed the fuck out. And, it made Blair turn wild. Her nipples had been extremely sensitive when she'd been pregnant with our son. I'd often made her come just from playing with them. But when she got pregnant with our daughter two months after Trevor was born, we'd discovered that knocked up and nursing was a lethal combination for Blair. I could give her orgasm after orgasm, right on the heels of each other by slamming my cock into her pregnant pussy and lavishing attention on her incredible breasts. So far, we'd gotten to five before she shoved me away and swore if I came near her again, she'd have her tubes tied after this baby.

I'd laughed because we both knew that pregnant Blair was horny all the time and she'd be begging for it soon enough. I was determined to get her to six one of these days.

"So?" she asked when we were sprawled out next to each other in bed, content and satisfied.

I grinned when I looked down to see her watching me through her lashes, twin pink spots blooming on her cheeks.

"There is no comparison," I declared quietly. "My fantasies have never lived up to the real thing."

Blair grinned and turned her head to kiss my chest, then raised her eyes to mine again. "What's the score now?"

I laughed and dragged her into my arms. "I've lost count, bunny." When Blair found my duffel of towels in the back of the town car one day, I ended up confessing to her about my morning fantasies. To my surprise, she wanted to know if she would trump my dreams of her. It came as no shock to me when she blew them away every single time.

"What's next?" she asked eagerly, and I chuckled.

"How about we stop trying to outdo what isn't real and focus on trying new things?"

Blair scratched her fingers down the whiskers on my face, making me shiver, and gave me a wicked grin. "Like the time we decided to see if the skin under your goatee was particularly sensitive?"

Yeah, turned out that was quite an erogenous zone for me. Go figure.

"How about we see if I can pump enough come into your pussy to turn this pregnancy into twins?" I teased.

"Good grief." She rolled her eyes playfully. "Then I'd be nursing two babies at once! My boobs would be huge!"

I cupped her tits and squeezed, then leaned down to lick them clean, making Blair moan. "Don't worry, bunny." I winked. "I'll eat their leftovers."

Blair arched her back, thrusting her breasts into my face and whimpered. "More," she begged.

Before I could give her what she wanted, a high-pitched wail came out of the baby monitor on the bedside table.

"Fuck," I groaned as I rested my forehead in the valley between her tits.

Blair giggled and moved to get out of bed, but I held her back with a hand on her shoulder. "Stay here, bunny. I'll bring him in."

After she fed the baby, we played with him until he fell back asleep. Blair and I watched him for a few minutes, enjoying the life we'd made for ourselves. I stood behind her with my hands resting on her growing belly. We only had around eight weeks left before we'd meet our daughter.

Once the doc gave her the "all clear" I was honest enough with myself to know that the Neanderthal wouldn't be too far in the shadows. She'd more than likely be bred again by the time our baby girl was three months old.

I removed one of my hands but kept the other on Blair's waist and guided her next door to our room. I flipped on the monitor and shut the door before going to work on removing Blair's clothes.

"About trying new things..." I trailed off, and she gave me a sassy look, making me laugh. "I'd like to get back to the attempt to turn one baby into two." I flashed her a cheesy grin, and she giggled.

"You just want to go for six," she argued.

"That should do it, don't' you think?"

Blair rolled her eyes. "I think five's my limit, babe."

I proved her wrong on two counts.

First, I got her to seven.

Second, it seemed turning one baby into two wasn't as impossible as it seemed.

After Blair delivered our daughter, the doctor blanched while looking at the computer screen, then yelled for the staff to get ready for another one.

They told us that little Jenna had been hiding Dani, and no one had realized it was twins until the birth.

I still maintained that it was the seventh orgasm.

EPILOGUE

BLAIR

Four and a half years later...

Watching Justice play with our children was one of my favorite things. He was such a great father. Justice was involved in every aspect of the kids' lives. K-Corp was more successful than ever, but he and Thatcher had quickly learned how to delegate to make time for what was important to them.

Justice even took over Trevor's t-ball team last year...after he got into it with the coach for supposedly flirting with me. I hadn't noticed anything inappropriate, but Justice insisted that the guy kept staring at me and had to go. I didn't argue since his possessive displays gave me a little thrill. It also didn't hurt that Trevor thought having his daddy as his coach was the best thing ever.

Of course, that led to his sisters complaining because Justice wasn't their coach too. The twins were four, and they weren't used to hearing no very often since they had their daddy and big brother wrapped around their little fingers. Rubbing my rounded belly, my lips curved up in a smile as I thought about how much Jenna and Dani had pestered their tumbling class teacher until she agreed that I could assist her.

But that had only lasted a few months before we found out we were expecting our fourth child. Justice tended to treat me like I was breakable when I was pregnant—except when he lost control in bed. And even then it was only to a certain extent. He didn't let go quite as much as normal.

Justice definitely didn't trust a bunch of rambunctious preschoolers to roll around on the mats with me. Especially not when he'd waited three years to knock me up again so I could finish my bachelor's degree. It'd been difficult with three babies at home, and I'd only managed it because of Justice's support. He wanted me to have everything I desired, and I'd learned early on in our relationship that he'd go to whatever lengths needed to make sure I got it. Not that he found taking the kids to the in-house daycare at K-Corp a hardship. Quite the contrary, he loved being able to pop in to see them throughout the day. And now that I was done with school, I was on site too because I'd taken over the running of the daycare so Pandora could retire. It was the perfect job for me, surrounded by kids—including all of my own until Trevor started kindergarten in the fall—and close to my husband.

"Help us get Daddy," the twins screeched in unison.

"Noooooo," Justice cried when Trevor switched sides and teamed up with the girls to reach up and tickle his sides and belly.

I'd been watching from the doorway of their playroom without any of them noticing me, but then a giggle slipped past my lips when Justice staggered backwards and crashed to the floor in an exaggerated fall. All four heads turned in my direction, and big grins split their precious faces.

"Wanna tickle Daddy, too?" Trevor offered, his

gray eyes twinkling with delight. "I'll hold him down so he can't get you back."

"Yeah, Dani and me can grab his arms," Jenna added, climbing over Justice's body to wrap her little hands around his left bicep.

Dani mirrored her action, throwing her body over Justice's right arm. "C'mon, Mommy! Get 'im!"

"How can I pass up an offer like that?" I laughed as I moved forward.

"Don't move, Daddy. We have to be careful with Mommy since she's pregnant," Trevor warned, mimicking what Justice had told the kids about a million times over the past few months as he held his legs down.

Justice craned his neck up to meet Trevor's gaze as he said, "Thanks for the reminder, buddy."

I barely held in my snort at Justice's response as I lowered myself to my knees next to him. He didn't need anyone to caution him when it came to me since he'd wrap me in bubble wrap if he could. And then I'd just have to get him all worked up until he couldn't wait to rip it right back off.

When my fingers brushed against his stomach before heading to his sides, Justice's eyes darkened to a stormy gray, and a low groan bubbled up his throat.

I couldn't torture him too much with the kids so close, but I also couldn't resist the temptation to cop a feel of his abs when they were right there in front of me. Not with my pregnancy hormones raging through my system, or at least that was the excuse I was going with.

Before we got any awkward questions about the sudden tightness of his jeans, I aimed for an especially ticklish spot just under his rib cage. When he roared with laughter, the kids wanted a turn too. By the time we were done, we were all laughing so hard that our sides hurt.

"Alright, guys. I think Mommy has had enough tickle time and needs a snack. How do cookies and milk sound to everyone?" Justice asked.

"Cookies! Yay!" the kids cheered, scrambling to their feet to race towards the kitchen.

"I'll get you back for that later," Justice murmured against my ear after helping me up from the floor so we could follow after them.

"You'd better," I whispered back with a wink, looking forward to some quality alone time when the kids went down for the night.

My life was better than I'd dreamed it would be in my wildest dreams about Justice. But just like he'd told me a million times about his fantasies, reality far surpassed my imagination.

Curious about Thatcher? Her Love is now available! And if you're in the mood for another taboo read, give The Virgin's Guardian a try!

THE VIRGIN'S GUARDIAN

One night.

One tiny lie.

It all comes back to bite me in the ass when my mysterious stranger shows up as my new guardian.

"C'mon, Felicity. You always say you're going to come with us, but you never actually do it."

Of course I didn't sneak out with Carrie to meet her friends. I only had a few months to go until I aged out of the foster system, and I didn't want to do anything to rock the boat. Carrie wasn't able to understand my fear since she didn't have to worry about getting kicked out. My foster parents were her real parents—something I hadn't had since I was ten and mine had died in a car crash. They'd both been only children of older parents, and they'd left home when their families had wanted them to get an abortion instead of having me way too young. With my parents gone, there had been nobody to take me in.

After being bounced around to a few different foster homes—a couple of which were decent, but one that wasn't—I'd come to live with Carrie's family when I was thirteen. Ever since then, I'd been on my best behavior, knowing that the safety I'd found there could be ripped from me at any moment.

"Felicity!" Carrie snapped, stomping her foot. "Are you even listening to me?"

"Yes," I lied.

"Then get up, get dressed, and put some make-up on."

"Carrie," I groaned, burying my head in my pillow.

"I don't want to hear it," she snapped. "My parents are going to be out super late tonight. They just left for dinner in downtown Seattle, and they're going to a late show with friends afterwards. You don't have any excuse not to come with me. They'll never even know we were gone."

I rolled over and looked up at her. She was probably right. Ever since she'd turned eighteen a month ago, they'd been a lot more lenient. Plus, the last time they'd done dinner and a show with friends, they hadn't made it home until after two o'clock in the morning. I'd been feeling a bit restless lately, so I decided to take the risk since it seemed minimal. "Fine. I'll go."

"And you'll let me pick out an outfit for you?" She blinked down at me with puppy-dog eyes.

If I was going to break the rules, I'd might as well do it looking my best. "Sure. Why not?"

It was a decision I came to regret an hour and a half later as I tugged the bottom of my dress while also trying to prevent my boobs from popping out of the top. "I cannot believe you talked me into wearing this dress."

She shrugged her shoulders. "It worked, didn't it? We look hot enough that they let us walk right in without asking for I.D."

"Yeah," I sighed, already wishing I'd just stayed home instead. I felt horribly out of place, even surrounded by Carrie and her friends. There were a lot more men than women in the bar, and everyone else looked like they belonged there. Even if we'd been twenty-one, we still would have been the youngest people there. Not that it stopped guys from sending us drinks. They were starting to pile up in on the table in front of me as I sipped at a diet soft drink.

"Then stop complaining and enjoy yourself," she

told me before she focused her attention back on her friends.

Their conversation drifted around me while I let my gaze sweep across the room. I wasn't paying much attention to what I was seeing until I noticed a guy staring at me. An insanely hot guy with hair so dark it looked almost black and eyes to match. Eyes that were heated and locked on my face.

"Holy shit," I breathed out. He was too far away to hear me, but his lips tilted up in humor as if he had. The dark scruff on his face didn't hide the smile.

I quickly looked away, unsure of how to react. Boys hit on me at school, but I'd never been tempted to do anything beyond innocent flirting. But this was no boy—he was all man. And just knowing he was watching me had me hot and bothered. I took a sip of my drink before I peeked up again and found him still staring at me. He was dressed in a three-piece suit that looked like it had been designed for his body. It probably cost twenty times more than the dress I was wearing. One that I'd had to borrow from Carrie.

I might have been young, but I wasn't dumb. I knew he was way out of my league. So, I gave him a little shake of my head, dragged my gaze away from him, and leaned over to whisper in Carrie's ear. "I'm not feeling very well. I'm heading to the bathroom, and then I'm going to grab an Uber home."

Her lack of empathy—and barely-there response—reminded me that although we'd lived under the same roof for more than four years, we weren't sisters. We were hardly even friends. If we had been, she would have insisted on coming with me, and I wouldn't have been alone when I walked out of the bathroom and right into a hard chest. Strong arms wrapped around me, and they didn't let go once I was steady on my feet again. I knew who they belonged to before I looked up.

"You can let go of me now," I whispered.

"I could," he agreed, his deep voice sending shivers down my spine. "But I'm not going to."

"That's going to be awkward since I'm ready to leave."

"Not awkward at all," he corrected. "It sounds like impeccable timing to me since I don't have anything keeping me here."

He didn't give me the opportunity to argue as he turned to lead me towards the front door. His arm slid down until his hand rested on my lower back.

"Alrighty then."

He chuckled and pulled me closer, completely unimpressed with my grumbling. When we stepped outside, he handed a ticket to the valet. The hundred dollar bill I saw tucked under it had me gasping. If I'd been the least bit unsure about how far outside my league this guy was, that would have convinced me. It would take me several babysitting gigs to make that much money.

"Do you need them to pull your car around, too?" he asked.

I lifted my cell out of my purse and wiggled it. "No, I was going to Uber home."

"Who brought you?" Those dark eyes of his flashed as he studied me.

My connection with Carrie was complicated, so I stuck with the simplest explanation. "One of the girls I was sitting with."

The valet pulled up in a black, two-door car. I didn't recognize the make or model, but it looked like something out of a movie. He left it running at the curb and opened the passenger side door.

"Oh, I'm not—" I started to explain.

A strong hand urged me forward as a deep voice whispered in my ear, "I'm more than happy to save you the hassle of waiting for an Uber."

"But—"

"You never know who's going to be behind the wheel of the car they send."

I swiveled on my heel, one hand on the frame of his car and the other on his chest. "I don't know you, either."

"Fuck. You're right," he groaned, digging into his suit jacket for his wallet. He flipped it open and pulled out his driver's license. "Here. Snap a picture of this and send it to your friend."

I did as he suggested, but I stopped short of actually sending the message. He'd calmed some of my fears by making the offer, and I didn't want to answer all the questions Carrie would have for me if she knew I'd left with a guy. Peering more closely at his ID, I noticed the date of birth. He wasn't just a guy; he was a thirty-seven-year-old man.

"Harrison Brooks, huh?" I asked once we were both settled in the car, and he was pulling away from the curb. "The name fits the car."

"You think so? I guess I'll take that as a compliment since I'm more than fond of my Vanquish." He quirked a dark eyebrow at me. "What about your name? Does it fit all the beauty that's you?"

"Pardon me?"

His husky laughter filled the car, but it felt nice. Not like he was making fun of me. "Your name, honey."

"Felicity."

"Felicity," he repeated, and my name had never sounded so good. "Perfect."

"Thanks," I whispered softly, my cheeks filling with heat.

"Which way am I headed?"

"Umm, hold on," I stammered. I didn't have my driver's license and wasn't familiar with the route Carrie had taken. As I was pulling my phone back out to pull up directions, my stomach growled. Loudly.

"Hitting the bar when you haven't eaten is never a good idea." He slowed the car and shot me another look. "Neither is leaving by yourself. You need to be more careful."

"I don't usually go to bars." The last thing I wanted to admit to him was how old I really was, so I didn't bother mentioning the reason. "And I did eat dinner, just not a lot of it."

His gaze swept downwards, lingering on my bare thighs below the short hemline of my dress. "It better not be because you're on a diet. You don't need it."

"Not a diet. Just not my favorite dinner." My foster mom made something I pretty much hated, so I'd barely eaten.

"Let me feed you before I drop you off."

"No, really. That's not necessary." My stomach

growled again, contradicting my words so I tried a different tactic. "You won't be able to find a restaurant open this late at night, and I can't picture you driving this car through a fast food drive-through."

He changed directions, doing a quick U-turn. "Challenge accepted, honey. I can have a hot meal in front of you in less than fifteen minutes."

AVAILABLE NOW!

ABOUT THE AUTHOR

The writing duo of Elle Christensen and Rochelle Paige team up under the Fiona Davenport pen name to bring you sexy, insta-love stories filled with alpha males. If you want a quick & dirty read with a guaranteed happily ever after, then give Fiona Davenport a try!